Words to Know Before You Read

appeared

gathering

giant

harp

magic

stalk

stranger

towered

vegetable

www.rourkepublishing.com

Edited by Luana K. Mitten
Illustrated by Helen Poole
Art Direction and Page Layout by Renee Brady

Library of Congress Cataloging-in-Publication Data

Koontz, Robin
 Jill and the Beanstalk / Robin Koontz.
     p. cm. -- (Little Birdie Books)
 ISBN 978-1-61741-811-2 (hard cover) (alk. paper)
 ISBN 978-1-61236-015-7 (soft cover)
 Library of Congress Control Number: 2011924662

Rourke Publishing
Printed in the United States of America, North Mankato, Minnesota
060711
060711CL

www.rourkepublishing.com - rourke@rourkepublishing.com
Post Office Box 643328 Vero Beach, Florida 32964

Jill and the Beanstalk

By Robin Koontz

Illustrated by Helen Poole

Jill grew a huge vegetable garden. One day a stranger appeared.

He asked for a bowl of soup. Jill gave him some vegetable soup.

"Here are some magic seeds for you," said the stranger. Jill thanked him and planted the seeds in her garden.

The next morning, a huge beanstalk towered high into the clouds.

Jill climbed up the stalk, gathering fresh beans.

8

Soon Jill saw a castle.
She heard singing
coming from inside.

Jill peeked inside the castle door. The singing was coming from a gold harp.

"Help me!" The harp cried when it saw Jill.

"Who is there?" yelled a loud voice.

A giant stomped into the room.
"I am sorry," said Jill. "I was picking beans and heard your singing harp."

"Beans? I love beans!"
said the giant.

13

"You may have all you want!" Jill said.

The giant gobbled down the beans that Jill gave him.

"My! These are sweet and tasty!" he said. "And since you love my harp, you may have it."

The giant handed the harp to Jill.

"And please, bring more beans when you have some to share," added the giant.

18

Before Jill climbed down the beanstalk, she thanked the giant for the harp and promised to make some bean treats for him.

19

"It is nice to share," said Jill as her new harp began to sing.

To Giant
Love Jill xxx

20

After Reading Activities

You and the Story...

How did Jill get the magic bean seeds?

Why did the giant give his harp to Jill?

Do you think Jill went back to visit the giant?

Think of a time you shared something with someone else. Tell what happened and how everyone felt.

Words You Know Now...

All the words listed below have little words in them. On a piece of paper write the big word and then circle the little word hidden inside of it.

appeared

gathering

giant

stalk

stranger

towered

vegetable

You Could... Plant a Garden of Your Own

- What will you plant in your new garden?

- Decide where you will plant your garden.

- Make a list of everything you will need.

- Write down everything you must do to take care of a garden.

- Imagine what would happen if some of the seeds you planted in your garden were magic. What would they grow into?

About the Author

Robin Koontz loves to write and illustrate stories that make kids laugh. Robin lives with her husband and various critters in the Coast Range mountains of western Oregon. She shares her office space with Jeep the dog, who gives her most of her ideas.

About the Illustrator

Helen Poole lives in Liverpool, England, with her fiancé. Over the past ten years she has worked as a Designer and Illustrator on books, toys, and games for many stores and publishers worldwide. Her favorite part of illustrating is character development. She loves creating fun, whimsical worlds with bright, vibrant colors. She gets her inspiration from everyday life and has her sketchbook with her at all times as inspiration often strikes in the unlikeliest of places!